GW00818573

THIS BOOK BELONGS TO

_____

_____

_____

PUFFIN BOOKS

UK | USA | Canada | Ireland | Australia
India | New Zealand | South Africa | China

Penguin Books is part of the Penguin Random House group of companies
whose addresses can be found at global.penguinrandomhouse.com.

Penguin
Random House
Australia

Published by Penguin Group (Australia), 2014

Printed and bound in Australia by Griffin Press, an accredited ISO AS/NZS 14001
Environmental Management Systems printer
National Library of Australia Cataloguing-in-Publication data available.
ISBN 978 0 14 330763 1

puffin.com.au
ouraustraliangirl.com.au

Charms on the front cover reproduced with kind permission from A&E Metal Merchants.
www.aemetal.com.au

OUR
AUSTRALIAN
GIRL

Meet Daisy

It's 1930, and Daisy lives on a farm, where she loves riding her horse, Jimmy, through the paddocks. Times are tough, and when her father loses his job, Daisy and her little sister, Flora, are sent to Melbourne to live with their aunt and uncle. Daisy must leave behind everyone she loves for a city she's never seen, and even her wildest daydreams can't prepare her for the new life that awaits . . .

Meet Daisy and join her adventure in the first of four exciting stories about a hopeful girl in troubled times.

Puffin Books

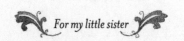 *For my little sister*

OUR
AUSTRALIAN
GIRL

Meet Daisy

Michelle Hamer

With illustrations by Lucia Masciullo

Puffin Books

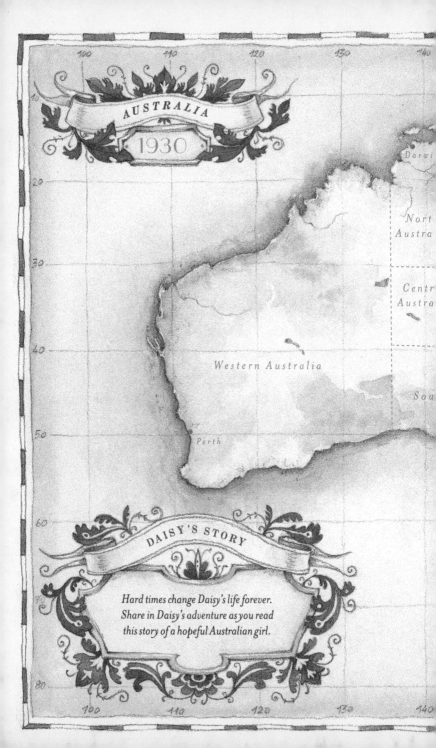

AUSTRALIA

1930

Darwi

*Nort
Austra*

*Cent
Austra*

Western Australia

Sou

Perth

DAISY'S STORY

*Hard times change Daisy's life forever.
Share in Daisy's adventure as you read
this story of a hopeful Australian girl.*

Where this story takes place

1
Bad News

DAISY grasped tighter to Jimmy's halter as the horse cantered through the paddock, mud flicking up from his hooves. His broad back was slick with rain and Daisy had to wrap her legs tightly around him.

'Ooh, Jimmy, you're doing that on purpose.' She laughed. 'I'm getting all muddy.'

The pony whinnied with pleasure and splashed through a big puddle, sending sheets of brown water all over Daisy.

'You're a terror,' she said, and slipped off Jimmy's back as he slowed down to a walk.

She wrapped her arms around his wide, brown neck. 'What am I going to do with you?' Jimmy nuzzled against her and Daisy felt his hot, sweet breath against her face.

A fine mist of rain was falling across the paddock and it was hard for Daisy to see the farmhouse through the haze. She realised she must have been riding for several hours. Time flew when she and Jimmy were racing through the wide, empty fields behind her house. Sometimes it felt like they were the only creatures on earth.

At least I've finally got a good ending for the play, Daisy thought, remembering what she'd come up with as she and Jimmy had thundered through the eerie bush behind their paddocks. And such an exciting, blood-curdling ending, too. Amelia will love it. I wonder if she's around.

Daisy walked Jimmy to the stable, ran a brush over his muddy flanks and made sure he had fresh hay and water, then picked the mud from his hooves and gave him a final kiss on the nose. 'See you in the morning, boy,' she said. 'Hopefully you can get us to school tomorrow without making us soaking wet.'

As she walked toward the house, Daisy saw through the gaps of the fence that her best friend, Amelia, was in the backyard next door.

'Hi, Amelia!' Daisy called. 'Shall we work on the play tonight? I came up with a *spine-chilling* ending while I was riding.' She rubbed her hands with glee. 'If we finish it tonight we can start rehearsals tomorrow after school.'

'Can't,' Amelia called back from the other side. 'I have to finish the darning or Mum won't let us use the front room to perform in again.'

They met at the gate between their gardens.

'Fair enough,' Daisy said. 'You'd better do a good job, though. We don't want to lose our only theatre. I'd *die* without acting.'

'Course I'll do a good job. My stitching is a

thousand times neater than yours, thank you very much. Anyway, I wanted to show you the tadpoles,' Amelia added, and held up a jar filled with murky water and tiny wriggling creatures. 'They grew legs today.'

'Ooh wonderful!' Daisy peered into the jar and sure enough several of the tadpoles had sprouted tiny black legs. 'We'll have to put them in the horse trough soon.'

'Maybe this time they'll stay there,' Amelia said, 'and we'll finally have a family of frogs.'

'You know they always end up hopping back over to the dam,' said Daisy. 'Anyway, remember my dad said if I bring home one more pet, he'll make me live out in the stable with them. He reckons two cats, a horse and a bunch of rowdy chooks is enough.'

Amelia laughed. 'Your dad always gives in, but I'll take these home just in case. See you in the morning. Don't forget Mrs Jamieson is giving us a maths test tomorrow.'

'How could I forget such *agony*?' Daisy said. She shook her head in dismay.

Amelia snorted. 'You're a goose.'

Daisy waved goodbye to her friend and skipped through the backyard, stopping to pet her one-eyed cat, Barnaby.

'Dad?' she called, slamming the wooden screen door behind her as she entered the kitchen, which was filled with the delicious smell of a rabbit pie.

'I'm here, love.' Daisy's father sat at the kitchen table his head bowed over a mug of tea. Her little sister, Flora, sat beside him.

'I was just going to call you in,' Dad said, and looked up at her with sad eyes.

Daisy immediately knew something was wrong and the happy feeling inside her evaporated. 'What is it, Dad? What's happened?'

He motioned for her to come and sit. Then, taking a deep sigh, he said, 'Girls, you know there've been no jobs here in Healesville for a long time. And since the stock market went bad and I got laid off, I haven't been able to pay the mortgage.' He laid his rough hands on the scrubbed kitchen table. 'I'm so sorry, girls, but the bank is taking the house off us. We have to leave the farm.'

Daisy felt cold all over. Without thinking, she put her arm around Flora, who hid her face in Daisy's chest. 'But Dad, this is our home! Are they allowed to do that?'

'The bank lent me the money to buy the house, love. I have to pay it back bit by bit every month, that's how a mortgage works. But if you can't pay, they take the house away and sell it to someone else.'

'Where will we live now?' Daisy asked, feeling her voice shake and her eyes fill with tears. She'd heard stories about families living in tents or sleeping in the park and Dad had even said that the banks had run out of money. It had all happened because of something called the stock-market crash, which she'd never really understood.

'I've thought about it, and there's only one thing to be done. You girls will go to stay with your Uncle Bertie and Aunty May in the city.'

'The city?' Daisy cried. 'But we've never even been to the city before! And I can't even remember what Uncle Bertie and Aunty May look like.' She pushed Flora gently away and rubbed her arms to chase off the chill that had settled on her. She tried to remember the aunt and uncle who had come to Mum's funeral just after Flora was born.

Then she realised that moving away meant being apart from Amelia, and her stomach felt tight and strange. 'And what about Jimmy?' she whispered. 'Can he come too?'

Dad shook his head sadly. 'No room for a horse in the city.'

'Can I bring the kitties?' asked Flora.

Dad shook his head again, and Flora started

to sniffle.

But suddenly an even worse thought hit her. 'What about you, Daddy? Won't you be with us?' Daisy looked at her father fearfully.

Dad slowly rubbed his hand across his mouth. 'Not at first, love,' he said quietly.

Daisy jumped up from her seat and her chair clattered noisily to the floor. 'But how will we manage without you? The city is full of gangsters and criminals! *Anything* could happen to us without you there.'

'Hold your horses now, Daisy, and calm down,' Dad said, picking up her chair. 'You're going to have to try not to be such a prima donna when you're at your aunty May's.'

Daisy hadn't understood what it meant the first time her dad had called her a prima donna, but he'd explained it was a name for the main lady in a play, and that people used the name to tease people when they got a bit carried away. Now Daisy was about to get cross – she hated being called that. But as she looked at Dad, she noticed that his grey eyes were rimmed with red and his forehead was furrowed with deep lines. She took a deep, shaky breath.

'The best way for us to be together again is if I can get some work, and the best way to do that is if I go on the track,' Dad said.

'What's the track?' asked Flora.

'It's the bush,' he explained. 'I've heard there's more work out there on the farms than in the towns.'

Oh, poor Dad, Daisy thought. She took a few more deep breaths to steady herself. I have to stop letting my imagination run away with me, she decided, and try to be brave, like a hero in a story. 'It will be an adventure, Flossy,' she said finally. 'We've never seen Melbourne before. We might get to see Luna Park and maybe we'll make some new friends.'

'Really?' Flora asked in a small voice and clutched tightly to her stuffed rabbit, Bunny.

'Sure we will,' Daisy said with a nod. As long as the gangsters don't get us, she thought to herself. She'd seen stories in the newspaper about the criminals in the city.

'That's the way,' Dad said and gave Daisy a tight smile. 'I'll write often, and I'll send for you girls as soon as I can.' Then he pulled them both into a strong hug. 'When I get regular work, I'll rent a place and we'll be together again. I promise.'

Daisy nodded, and snuggled into his big warm chest, breathing in his familiar smell of freshly dug earth and tobacco.

But inside she felt as though she'd been tipped upside down in a carnival ride; her stomach churned and her thoughts were scrambled. How could they live with people who were practically strangers in the middle of the busy city? And how could she possibly stand being away from Jimmy and Amelia?

'When will we have to leave?' she asked.

Daisy felt her dad swallow. 'Saturday.'

Saturday? That was only three days away! Daisy felt more tears welling up inside her that she didn't want Flora to see.

She leapt up and rushed back outside into the biting winter air, through the maze of fruit trees, among the chickens, who squawked in annoyance, and under the sagging wooden fence to Jimmy's stable.

She flung her arms around his neck and let herself sob into his thick, black mane. The horse seemed to sense her sadness and whinnied gently in her hair.

'I love you, Jimmy,' she whispered into his ear. He bobbed his neck in return and butted her gently in the chest with his nose. 'I don't want to go to the city away from everyone I love. I'm going to miss you so much.'

Almost unable to see where she was going through her tears, Daisy ran into Amelia's backyard.

'But when do you have to leave?' Amelia asked, her eyes growing round in her freckled face as the two friends sat before the glowing kitchen fire.

'Saturday,' Daisy said, a sick feeling rising in her tummy. 'Will you look after Jimmy for me? Dad says there won't be any room for a horse in the city.'

'Of course, and the cats and chooks,' Amelia said. 'But I don't want you to go.' A tear ran down her cheek. 'I can't imagine not seeing you every day. What about our play, and the tadpoles, and school? Who will I sit with now?'

'I don't know,' Daisy replied sadly. 'But we'll still stay best friends, right?'

'Yep,' Amelia said, and chewed thoughtfully on the end of one of her long blonde plaits. 'Geez, you'll miss your dad though, won't you? What will you do without him?'

'I don't know. I'm really scared,' Daisy admitted, and her chin started wobbling. 'But he's going to write lots and hopefully we won't have to be apart for too long.'

'Well, I'll write, too – every week, every single week,' Amelia said, her blue eyes darkening with determination. 'And we'll never, ever forget each other, cross our hearts and hope to die.' She looked at Daisy solemnly, and they quietly ran their fingers over their hearts, spat on their palms and shook hands.

Three days later, Daisy and Flora said a tearful goodbye to their father at the train station.

The morning was bitterly cold. Daisy's breath hung in a fog around her mouth and her fingers were blue. The station was quiet, with just a few passengers on the platform, tapping their feet and puffing on their hands for warmth.

'Now remember,' Dad said, 'I'll write as often as I can, and send money to help Aunty May and Uncle Bertie.'

'Promise?' Daisy said, gripping his arm.

'Of course, love,' he said.

He handed her a small bundle of cold roast potatoes tied up in an old tea towel. Daisy had watched yesterday as he'd tumbled the spuds from the earth. She never grew tired of watching him pluck food from the dirt as if by magic.

I wonder what we'll eat in the city, Daisy thought, chewing her lip. Do they even have vegie gardens there? She tucked the lunch under her arm, gave her dad a last tight hug, then led Flora onto the carriage and settled her on a seat.

She squashed a pillowcase containing their few belongings into the luggage rack above them. The train began to vibrate as the engine warmed up, its sliding doors rattling against the carriages.

Before the train started to move, Daisy heard someone yelling her name. She pulled open the window and saw Amelia running down the platform.

'Daisy, Daisy, wait!' she called. She finally reached Daisy's window as the guard blew his whistle. 'For you,' she cried, forcing a small package into Daisy's hand as the train began to move slowly down the tracks.

'Goodbye, Amelia, I'll write soon. I love you, Daddy. Goodbye!' Daisy shouted, waving madly from the window until the two figures on the platform were just specks.

She pulled the window closed again, feeling her cheeks burn from the sharp morning air. She looked at the brown paper parcel in her hand and her chest hurt again. She put it safely in her pocket to open later. It would be nice to have something to look forward to in her new home.

2
The Big City

ESPITE Daisy's sadness at leaving her home, soon she couldn't help but be excited by her first train journey.

She watched in wonder as the landscape zipped by her window. Endless fields of green grass, then vegetables, then busy streets appeared and disappeared beyond the glass. Dribbles of rain ran down the window and far off in the distance she could see lightning flashing over the hills.

The train stopped at stations to let passengers on and off. Flora soon lay on the seat and fell asleep, and Daisy was left to her own thoughts. Maybe living in the city *would* be an adventure. Aunty May and Uncle Bertie might even have time to take them to the Melbourne Zoo to ride Queenie the elephant. There'd been a photo in the newspaper of children having a ride on her. How exciting that would be, to sit on top of an elephant!

Oh, and maybe they'd even have a cat, or a dog. That would make the city feel more like home. She thought of the two cats they'd had since they were tiny kittens, Barnaby and Jess, and her heart ached all over again.

At Drysdale a well-dressed woman got on board with two young boys, who danced and chased around her skirts.

'Calm down, boys,' she scolded, but her sons ignored her.

Daisy watched the lady move down the

carriage. She has such lovely clothes, Daisy thought, trying not to stare at the woman's elegant velvet jacket and dainty lilac hat.

She looked down at her own simple dress. Amelia's mother had made it last summer from an old flour sack. Her coat was an ugly, scratchy brown thing made from scraps of hessian. Daisy tried to imagine how warm and soft a velvet coat would feel around her. I wonder if Aunty May has one I could try on, she thought excitedly. Ooh, and maybe some hats with flowers on them that me and Flora could dress up in. Maybe I'll write a new play and we can use Aunty May's old clothes as costumes.

Her happy daydream was interrupted when one of the lady's sons suddenly ran toward the door of the carriage. Just as the train began to sway and pick up speed, he put his hand on the door as if to open it.

'Stop, you'll fall out,' Daisy cried, fear fizzing up inside her. She leapt from her seat and grabbed the boy around the waist just as he succeeded in sliding the door open.

'Oscar!' his mother screamed as the train lurched around a bend and the boy came dangerously close to toppling out onto the tracks below.

Daisy turned and grabbed a leather strap hanging from the ceiling as the ground rushed past her eyes. She grunted with the effort of pulling herself and the boy back into the carriage with one arm on the strap and the other around the boy's squirming waist.

A man reached over and slammed the door closed as Daisy and the boy sprawled onto the floor of the carriage.

Daisy could hardly breathe. Her heart was pounding. The boy ran off down the train.

'Are you all right?' the man asked, helping Daisy off the floor.

'Yes, I think so,' she said, though she was still shaking.

The boy's mother rushed up, her face pale with shock. 'Oh my dear, thank you so much – that was very brave of you. You saved Oscar's life. How can I ever thank you?'

'There's no need,' Daisy said, feeling her cheeks turn red.

Flora ran over and wrapped herself around Daisy's legs. 'Daisy, you scared me,' she cried.

'How old are you, dear?' the lady asked.

'Eleven,' Daisy answered.

'Well, what a capable girl you are. Your parents must be very proud of you.'

Daisy felt herself blush even deeper. 'Well, it's just our dad now. Our mother died when my sister was born.' Even though it had happened six years ago, Daisy still felt her throat close up when she talked about it.

'Oh my dear, I'm sorry to hear that. You must let me treat you to afternoon tea when we get to the city,' the woman said. 'My name is Mrs Johnson. The least I can do is buy you some tea and a scone.'

'Thank you, Mrs Johnson,' Daisy replied, 'but our Aunty May is going to meet us at the station. We're going to stay with her for a while.'

'All right then, dear, but make sure you tell her how brave you were,' Mrs Johnson said. 'I dare say she will want to take you out for a treat herself.' She squeezed Daisy's hand and went back to her children.

Daisy led Flora back to their seats. I hope Aunty May is exactly like her, she thought. And I can't wait to tell Amelia how I almost *died*.

A few hours later, Daisy and Flora were standing on the platform inside Flinders Street Station. They stared up at the towering ceilings, feeling stunned by the bustling crowds and the toots and whistles from departing and arriving trains.

It's like being inside a giant ant's nest, Daisy thought. But instead of dirt, the nest was made of concrete and steel and glass. There was so much to look at that she swivelled her head from side to side and turned around on the spot several times trying to take everything in, until finally she grew dizzy and had to stand still.

Flora pressed close to her sister. Neither of them had ever been inside such an enormous building. Daisy felt very small as she looked through the crowd for someone who might be Aunty May. Dad had said she was tall and thin with long hair.

A smiling woman wearing a fur and a jaunty red hat came towards them. That's her! Oh, she looks lovely, Daisy thought. I wonder if she'll let me try her fur on when we get home? Maybe she's made a cake to welcome us to the city? Daisy smiled widely, but the woman walked right past.

Suddenly a stern-faced woman with

pinched cheeks and a pointy nose came up to them. Her beady eyes reminded Daisy of a hungry crow. 'You'll be Daisy and Flora, I'd imagine,' she said, hardly glancing at them.

'Ye-es,' Daisy said. 'Are you Aunty May?' All her thoughts of pretty clothes and cake evaporated.

'Well, I'm not the King's wife now, am I?' the woman snapped, and without another word led the sisters through the crowded station and out into the city.

She's horrible, Daisy thought, her shoulders drooping with disappointment. But then her father's sad eyes came into her mind. 'Buck up,' she whispered to herself, and squeezed Flora's hand tighter.

Out on the pavement Daisy's eyes widened with amazement. Flinders Street Station, with its grand domed roof, sat at the intersection of several busy city roads where cars, trams and pedestrians jostled for space.

Daisy blinked as cars zipped past, sometimes two at a time with trams in between them. But it's not dirty and scary at all, she thought with surprise. Instead of the green fields and trees of home, there were buildings and roads, but all the energy and activity delighted her. Maybe I can be part country-girl, part city-girl, Daisy thought.

'Goodness me, Flossy, isn't it all so busy?' Daisy exclaimed over the clang of the trams, hum of engines, car horns and shouts of people in the streets. She could feel her pulse racing with the excitement of it all and longed to explore the streets.

A group of schoolgirls rushed past them, laughing and joking loudly. They look so smart in their uniforms, Daisy thought. They even have hats and gloves. It will be thrilling to go to school in the city!

Suddenly she realised Aunty May had rushed ahead, so she gave Flora a gentle shake and they walked quickly after her.

Aunty May wove in and out of the crowded footpath impatiently. Only when she reached the edge of the wide road did she stop and look back for them. 'Come on, come on,' she said. 'We don't have time for sight-seeing. I have the dinner to see to, and goodness knows I'll have my work cut out for me now.' Her small eyes flicked over the sisters.

Daisy reached down to put her arm around Flora. 'We'll be no trouble, Aunty May.'

'Hmph,' Aunty May replied, and, seeing a break in the traffic, strutted across the road.

She doesn't want us here, Daisy realised, and her stomach lurched with fear. This is going to be much worse than I thought.

Flora looked up at Daisy with tears in her eyes. 'It's so busy. I don't like it,' she said. 'I want to go home.'

Daisy wiped the frown from her face, and gave Flora a smile. 'I know, Flossy, but look at those buildings – did you ever see anything so big in your life?' She pointed at a beautiful cathedral in front of them, its many spires reaching into the cloudy sky.

Flora tilted her head to see the top. 'I still want to go home. I want Daddy,' she said, and chewed forlornly on Bunny's ears.

'Girls!' Aunty May shouted from the other side of the road.

Daisy jolted into action. She didn't want to make Aunty May any crosser. She grabbed Flora's arm and dragged her quickly toward the road. Just as she was about to step off the gutter, a truck whooshed past, spraying the sisters with muddy water. The driver blew his horn loudly at them.

Daisy's heart thumped hard in her chest. She hugged Flora tight. 'I'm so sorry, Flossy, I wasn't concentrating,' she said. Oh my goodness, she thought to herself. It's only our first day here and I nearly had us both squashed under the wheels of a truck! We could have been *killed*.

Suddenly Aunty May was beside them. 'What are you girls playing at? I'll not be kept waiting like this,' she said, then paused as she took in their mud-spattered clothes.

Daisy looked at Flora's face, which was speckled with mud, her hair bow turned sideways so that it seemed to be coming out of her ear, and couldn't help but giggle at the funny sight she made.

'You think this is amusing, do you, my girl?' Aunty May said, her face turning red with anger. 'Well, I'm not accustomed to such rudeness nor such dreadful behaviour. I am already regretting taking you two on. We may be in reduced circumstances, but we still have standards.'

She pulled her shabby coat tightly around her and adjusted the tortoiseshell comb that held her grey bun in place.

'I'm sorry, Aunty May,' Daisy said, her

voice shrinking inside her.

She tried hard to stay beside her aunt for the rest of the long walk.

By the time they reached Aunty May and Uncle Bertie's tumbledown cottage in a dirty city laneway, Daisy's arm was aching from carrying their belongings, and Flora was whimpering with tiredness and hunger.

Aunty May pushed the battered front door open, revealing a dark room.

'Shoes at the door,' she ordered, before padding inside.

Daisy slipped her boots off quickly while Flora sat down on the floor to pull hers off.

Daisy could smell sour milk and dampness in the cold house. Wind whined at the windows and swept down the empty fireplace, fluttering the yellowed kitchen curtain. In the middle of the room sat a table laid with three plates. There was a kitchen dresser on one wall, with a collection of mismatched crockery. Cold air whistled between gaps in the creaking floorboards.

What a miserable place! Daisy thought. It's so cold and dark, like a troll's house under a bridge. She thought back to their cosy farmhouse and her chest suddenly felt tight. She hugged her arms around her body and tucked her chin onto her chest, letting her long hair fall around her head like a curtain. It was almost like being in a warm cave.

Aunty May struck a match and lit a kerosene lantern that created a small pool of light. She pointed to a tiny room off the kitchen. 'Put your things in there,' she said, pulling Daisy out of her thoughts.

Daisy put the pillowcase on a faded couch in the lounge room. She noticed the paint was peeling from the walls and a large patch of mould was growing on the ceiling.

A set of framed photos on a shelf caught her eye. 'Is this you, Aunty May?' Daisy asked, peering at the photo of a young woman in a beautiful ball dress. Another showed a grand mansion with 'Somers 1912' written on the photograph. 'Where was this?'

'Stay away from what doesn't belong to you,' Aunty May snapped as she came into the room. 'That's a memory of a better time, no point thinking about it now. And stop asking questions. Children should be seen and not heard.'

Geez, she really is awful! Daisy thought. But she looks so pretty in the photograph. I wonder how she got so unhappy.

'Now come and wash your hands for dinner before your uncle gets home. He won't want the likes of you bothering him.' Aunty May cocked her head toward the back door. 'Tap's outside the door, the lavvy is up the back.'

Daisy helped Flora wash her hands and did

her best to wipe the mud off her sister's face in the freezing tap water.

The stale bread and cold mutton Aunty May put out for them tasted wonderful after the long day. Daisy washed her food down with a cup of sweet tea.

Suddenly the front door banged open and a raspy voice called, 'Hey, guess who's home?'

Daisy stood up as her uncle Bertie burst into the room. 'Ah, so these are the lovely girlies, are they then?' he said, a big smile spreading across his face.

He came up to Daisy and reached behind her. 'What's this, then?' he asked, seemingly pulling a penny out of her hair. 'Do you always keep your coins behind your ears?'

Daisy couldn't help but laugh. Thank goodness Uncle Bertie wasn't as cross as his wife, she thought.

'Now now, Bertie, that's enough of the theatrics,' Aunty May scolded, and banged another plate of mutton and bread on the table.

Daisy realised Flora was staring at the stump of Uncle Bertie's missing arm. She nudged her sister.

'No harm done,' Uncle Bertie said in his gravelly voice, noticing Flora's stare. He grabbed the stump with his good arm. 'That's what the war did to me, girls, that and me lungs. Burned and useless from the mustard gas they are – that's why me voice is all scratched up.'

Daisy wasn't sure what mustard gas was, but it certainly sounded terrible. 'I'm Daisy,' she said, 'and this is Flora. Our dad told us that you lost your arm in the war.'

'Lost it? Lost it?' Uncle Bertie cried, tucking into his dinner with gusto. 'Makes it sound like a man misplaced the thing.'

Daisy giggled again. She liked her uncle already.

'I didn't lose it, girls. The darn thing was

blown off by a grenade. I saw me arm fly right past me nose. I knew where it was all right, it just wasn't on me body anymore.' He laughed loudly, slapping his hand on his knee.

I wonder if it hurt a lot, Daisy thought, but stayed quiet in case the question was rude. Still, it was a thrilling story.

'Do you still work at the war?' Flora asked.

'What, girl? Didn't anyone tell you? The war's been over for a good ten years now,' he said. 'It's just battered blokes like me wandering around that remind anybody of it.'

'Your uncle just got a job working three days a week at The Myer Emporium, Flora. It's the best store in the city,' Aunty May cut in. 'He's an elevator operator. Soon we'll have enough money to move out of this dreadful slum and into a proper house in a better suburb.'

'Nothing wrong with Gertrude Street,' Uncle Bertie said, and gave Daisy a big wink.

'Don't you believe what the papers say about crime and other goings-on. It's a good place.'

Aunty May ignored him. 'Before the war your uncle worked at the bank. He was well on his way to becoming the manager.' She picked up her chipped cup and sipped her tea through pursed lips.

Daisy thought she saw a shadow pass over Uncle Bertie's eyes, but he quickly smiled it away. 'Thank God I got outta that place, girls. A man would have died of boredom.'

'Nonsense,' snapped Aunty May. 'If it wasn't for the war, we'd be living somewhere a lot more respectable.'

Ahhh, I understand, Daisy thought. Aunty May was going to be a bank manager's wife in a fancy house. No wonder she's so grumpy. I suppose that is a bit tragic.

Aunty May got up from the table and began banging dishes in the sink noisily. 'Right then, Daisy, you can dry up, and you, Flora, you can clear the table. Hurry up now.'

Daisy rushed over to help. She picked up a tea towel and stood beside Aunty May at the sink. 'Umm, Aunty May, I was just wondering . . . when will Flora and I be starting school?' she asked.

'School? School?' Aunty May replied in a shrill voice. 'Isn't it enough that we're giving you a roof over your heads?'

Daisy slowly picked up a plate and wiped it.

'No, there will be no school,' Aunty May continued. 'I don't want your father thinking this is a permanent situation. No need for you girls to get too settled.' She angrily flicked a piece of gristle off the plate she was holding.

We may as well be living in a dungeon, Daisy thought gloomily. Being stuck inside with Aunty May all day and not going to school will be like *torture*.

Daisy and Flora were soon cuddled up on the couch, a thin blanket barely covering them. It was cold and everything felt wrong without Dad sitting by the fireside while they drifted off to sleep. Daisy blinked back quiet tears as Flora snored beside her.

Dear Amelia, she imagined herself writing. *You'll think I'm being dramatic, but we really are the prisoners of an evil witch, forced to sleep in a freezing dungeon . . .*

Something clicked in Daisy's memory and she wriggled out from Flora's grasp, leapt off the couch and picked up her jacket from the back of a chair. She thrust her hand into the pocket and pulled out the package that Amelia had passed her through the train window. In all the drama of the day, she had forgotten about it till now.

Pulling off the string, she carefully opened the packet and gasped with delight. 'Oh, Jimmy!' she whispered, staring at a photograph of her beautiful horse. She read the note that

Amelia had tucked inside the package.

'*Dear Daisy, I was saving this for your birthday, but I thought you might need to have it in the city. Doesn't Jimmy look fine standing in the sunshine?*

Your friend forever, Amelia xxx'

Happy tears now slid down Daisy's cheek as she stared at the photo, which showed Jimmy standing in his paddock, his head cocked to one side. She knew Amelia's uncle was a keen photographer. She must have secretly got him to take the photo. A small bundle dropped out of the brown paper. What's this? Daisy wondered. As she picked it up, she realised it was a thin bunch of horsehair tied with string. Amelia had trimmed a piece of Jimmy's mane.

Daisy breathed in the familiar horsey smell and smiled at the photograph. It was almost like having Jimmy here with her. How she wished she was in her own bed with Barnaby and Jess curled up on her feet, Jimmy just out the back in his stable and Dad in the next room.

3
New Friends

DAISY spread cold fat onto a slice of bread, boiled water on the stove to make tea and then called Flora in from the backyard for breakfast. 'Quickly, Flossy! I want to get going.'

'Going where?' Aunty May asked, looking up from her darning.

In the ten days that Daisy had been in the city, Aunty May had kept her busy doing chores in the house, but today Daisy wanted to explore beyond their crowded laneway. Perhaps being out and about would help her throw off the sadness that had seemed to cover her like a heavy blanket since they'd arrived. She'd hoped her homesickness would get better, but she still cried herself to sleep every night. Aunty May was forever telling Daisy what to do, as if she was only a little kid.

'I thought I might take a look around,' Daisy said. 'Explore a little. I don't need you to come with me,' she added hurriedly. 'I'm quite used to going places myself.'

'Well, the cheek!' Aunty May's face flushed with anger. 'You'll do no such –'

'I made a friend,' Flora announced as she ran in, banging the door loudly behind her.

'For pity's sake, child, learn some manners,' said Aunty May. 'It's too late for your sister, but there's still hope for you to grow up as a lady, you know.'

Flora ran to hide behind Daisy.

'I'm sorry, Aunty,' Daisy said through gritted teeth. 'I'm sure Flora will be more careful in the future.'

Aunty May snorted loudly. 'I doubt that very much,' she said. 'It seems your father let you run wild out there in the country.'

A bolt of anger surged through Daisy. 'Our dad is the best dad in the world!' she said angrily, putting her hands on her hips.

'Is that so?' Aunty May responded. 'Then why hasn't he sent any money for your keep, or even a letter in almost two weeks?'

'I'm sure he has,' Daisy spluttered. 'It . . . it must have got lost in the mail. I'm sure it will come today.' She twisted the tea towel into a tight coil. It was true. Two long, chatty letters had come from Amelia, but they hadn't heard one word from Dad. He wouldn't have forgotten – I know he wouldn't, Daisy thought. But she couldn't stop a nagging worry at the back of her mind.

'I won't be holding my breath,' Aunty May said sourly, tapping her yellowed fingers on the table. 'But I'll tell you this: I won't be spending a penny more on you than he provides, understand? Me and Bert are putting every farthing aside for our new home. I can't be wasting money on someone else's children.'

'I know, Aunty May, you told me already,' Daisy said tightly, dipping her eyes to stare at the splintered cracks in the floorboards, where she could hear rats scurrying at night.

'Don't you dare answer back!' Aunty May's eyes grew cold and hard as she spoke. 'You're of an age to work. So unless your father comes good and sharpish, that's what you're going to have to do. Or we'll have to make . . . other arrangements.'

Flora hugged into Daisy even tighter, and Daisy's head throbbed with worry. Surely she wouldn't force them to live on the streets? How dare she suggest it! Uncle Bertie would never allow that . . . would he?

Aunty May picked up her purse and a string bag. 'Right, I'm off to the shops to see what we can manage for dinner.' She jingled a few coins in her hand. 'See you don't get into any mischief. And Daisy, you're not to go anywhere while I'm out. I forbid it.'

What a nasty piece of work! Daisy thought hotly as she watched her aunt leave. And who's she to tell me what to do when I've been looking after us just fine all these years? 'Never mind,' she said to Flora. 'She's just trying to scare us. Now come and sit at the table, and tell me about your friend.'

'Oooh she's ever so nice,' Flora said, her eyes shining happily. 'But Daisy, her eyes look different to ours, and her hair is so black and shiny. Her name's Yi Le. We helped her mum do the washing. Her mum said they used to live in a place called China. Then they had a vegie shop, but it got closed when no one had any money. Oh, and her mum talks in a funny language, but Yi Le knows what she's saying.' Flora stopped to take a bite of her bread.

'Goodness, you certainly know a lot about them already.' Daisy laughed. She reached out to smooth Flora's scruffy hair.

Flora gulped the last of her breakfast. 'Can I go? Me and Yi Le are gonna make mud pies.'

'All right,' Daisy agreed, 'but mind you stay at her house and don't go wandering.'

'I promise.' Flora ran out the back door, slamming it behind her once again.

Daisy winced. At least Aunty May wasn't there to tell Flora off.

With the house empty, she had time to think about their predicament. She couldn't think why they'd heard nothing from Dad yet. The little bit of money he'd given Aunty May was almost gone.

But surely she wouldn't really throw us out on the streets? Daisy picked at some crumbs on Flora's plate. There was already barely enough food for her little sister, and a couple of days ago, Daisy had started giving most of

her meals to Flora because Aunty May made
them so small. She'd missed dinner last night
and breakfast this morning already, and her
stomach rumbled uncomfortably. What if she
starved to death before Dad's letter came? She
imagined herself lying pale and thin on the
floor of the cottage as she whispered her final
goodbyes to Flora.

Daisy shook her head. Don't be such a prima
donna, she reminded herself. Of course a letter
with some more money would arrive any day,
and then Aunty May wouldn't be so mean.

With that comforting thought she cleared
up the breakfast things and then pulled on her
boots and jacket and stepped into the narrow
laneway outside the front door. I'll go and
have a quick poke around, she decided. And if
Aunty May beats me home, well, I'll just tell
her I was out watching for the postman.

She walked past the now-familiar row
of cottages crowded beside Aunty May and

Uncle Bertie's, most with patched roofs, broken fences and smashed windows boarded up with scraps of wood.

Everything looks so sad and broken, Daisy thought. It's like nobody cares about this place at all. At home people took pride in their gardens and houses.

She wandered up the laneway, where children sat playing on the bricks, women stood at their front doors washing clothes in big metal tubs and skinny dogs sniffed for food scraps. Two girls were skipping with an old rope a few houses away, singing loudly as they took turns to jump.

'Elsie, that's two verses. It's my turn,' one of them shouted.

As Daisy grew closer she realised the girls were twins. They each had wild, curly black hair tangled around their pale faces, and eyes as dark as coal, with long, thick lashes.

One of the girls gave Daisy a cheery wave.

'Hello,' she said. 'Want to play skippy? If Elsie would ever let anyone have a turn.'

Elsie stopped skipping and threw the rope to her sister. 'Geez, you could whinge the leg off a black dog, you could, Mabel,' she said.

Daisy noticed that each sister had one bare foot. 'Why are you only wearing one shoe?'

Elsie shrugged. 'We've got two shoes and four feet.'

'We used to take turns of having the whole pair for a day,' Mabel added. 'But we reckon sharing is better.'

'But we swap feet at midday, so the blisters stay even,' Elsie finished.

'Oh,' Daisy said. 'And do you always finish each other's sentences?'

'Always,' the twins said together, their faces breaking into identical grins.

Daisy laughed. 'I'm Daisy. I'm visiting from the country.'

'Visiting, eh? Well, we could show you

round the city,' Elsie offered. 'Oh, and I'm Elsie, and she's Mabel, but it doesn't really matter. We answer to both names seeing most people get us confused.'

'I'll try to get your names right,' Daisy said, 'and I'd love to see the city. I can't be too long, though. My aunt will be back soon.'

'Righto,' the twins said in unison. They each linked an arm through Daisy's and led her down the lane. It felt nice to walk between them.

'You've even got matching dresses,' Daisy said. She looked at their drab grey smocks.

'Yeah, Susso dresses,' Elsie said.

'What does Susso mean?' Daisy asked. She'd never heard the word before.

They'd reached a main road at the end of the lane and the twins stopped to check for traffic.

'Our dad gets help 'cos there's no jobs. That's what the Susso is — money and food and that. The Susso blokes do work for the government,' Mabel explained. 'Our dad's helping to build a shrine for the soldiers killed in the war.'

'But he only gets a few bob,' Elsie said. She led them across the road. 'They give us clothes and stuff, too.' She looked at her one bare foot and laughed. 'But not enough of anything, really.'

They walked on until they reached a park filled with well-tended flower beds and tall elm trees. 'So this is the Fitzroy Gardens,' Elsie continued, and waved her arm around her.

'Me and Elsie pick wildflowers here,' said Mabel, 'but you have to be careful of the gardener. He's got a real mean streak. We sell bunches in the springtime.'

'But not this spring. We just started working at the pickle factory so we'll soon be wearing fancy furs and dripping with diamonds,' said Elsie. 'We'll be real posh, won't we, Mabel?'

'Oh yes, and then we'll buy a big shiny car

and as much food as we like,' Mabel said.

'What about school?' Daisy asked.

'We left a month ago when we turned thirteen.' Mabel ran off to fling herself into a series of wild cartwheels across the wet grass.

Daisy watched as Mabel's shoe went flying into a hedge. Maybe I *could* get a job, she thought, twisting a length of her hair and trying to ignore the hunger pangs in her stomach. Then Aunty May couldn't make us leave, and maybe Dad could come back here and we could all be together. 'Are there any more jobs at the pickle factory?'

'Maybe,' Elsie said. 'But how old are you?'

'Eleven.'

'I reckon you'd have to say that you were twelve, otherwise they might not think you're up to it. And it's no picnic, you know. It's hot, back-breaking work.'

Daisy nodded but her mind was racing with plans. I'll get a job straight away and buy lots of food, and give money to Aunty May, and maybe I can even arrange for Flora to go to school, and . . . Ouch! She'd been twisting her hair so frantically she didn't realise she'd made a big knot.

'You right there, country girl?' Elsie laughed as Daisy tried to untangle her finger.

Daisy blushed and nodded. 'Have you two always lived in Melbourne?' she asked.

'Yep, we were born right there in Gertrude Street,' Elsie said, bending to pick some dandelions from the grass. 'There's three more after us, all boys, which is an awful pain. Boys are such a nuisance.'

'Right then,' Mabel came puffing up to them with twigs and leaves stuck in her hair and her boot back on her foot. 'It's time for a spot of morning tea, I think.'

'Shall we go to the usual place, my dear?' Elsie asked, using a posh accent and curtseying to her sister.

'Oh, do let's,' Mabel answered with a giggle and, tucking her arm into Daisy's again, began skipping.

The twins would be perfect in one of my plays, Daisy thought as they crossed the park and wove through the back streets and laneways of the city, past furniture makers and laundries, haberdashery shops and boot menders.

Soon they came to a part of the city that was very different to Gertrude Street. There were fancy shops with glass windows and people wearing expensive-looking clothes. The ladies wore smart coats and gloves, and the men were in suits with stylish hats. Daisy thought they looked marvellous.

'This is where the rich people shop,' Mabel told her. 'We like to come and look at all the fancy things.'

If I get a job, Flora and I could come here and have tea, Daisy thought. I'd buy us satin dresses and we'd wear lacey gloves and pretend we were the daughters of a millionaire.

They reached a large white building that sprawled across a wide stretch of the street taking up the space of many shops. Daisy read the name across the top of the building: *The Myer Emporium.* 'My uncle Bertie works here!' she told the twins. 'I'm going in to say hello.' As she pushed through the store's large glass doors the twins anxiously called for her to come back, but Daisy was sure Uncle Bertie would be pleased to see her so she walked right in.

Suddenly the noise of the street fell away, and with it the grime and weariness of the city. Daisy tried to work out where the soft music was coming from, but there were no musicians to be seen.

It looks like fairyland, Daisy thought as she took in the pretty glass bottles on shiny counters, silk scarves in boxes on a shelf, a display of hats in a rainbow of colors and pots of make-up beside gleaming mirrors.

Her dirty boots looked out of place on the polished timber floor and she quickly tried to smooth down her hair.

A man in a smart red jacket came up to her. 'I don't think we have what you're looking for, Miss,' he said, his lips curling at the edges.

'Pardon?' Daisy answered in confusion.

'I think you must be lost,' the man said, taking her arm and steering her back out the door.

'Oh no, I . . . my uncle . . .' Daisy stuttered, but before she could finish she found herself being whisked outside.

Back on the noisy street the man stared down at her with a frown. 'There's nothing here for the likes of you,' he said and stalked back into the store.

'Oh Daisy, are you all right?' The twins were sympathetic. 'We tried to warn you that they wouldn't let you in,' Mabel said, 'but you dashed away so fast.'

'Never mind.' Daisy tossed her head. 'Just promise me that when you girls get rich you never shop there.' Her cheeks were hot with embarrassment.

'We'll buy our furs somewhere else,' Elsie said with a giggle.

'Ooh look, anyway, this is where I'll be spending my fortune.' Elsie pointed to a sweet shop a few doors away.

Daisy peered through the window and saw a group of girls in pretty dresses choosing boiled sweets from big glass jars. Each time one of them pointed at a jar, the shopkeeper unscrewed the lid and poured a small scoop of the colorful sweets into an already bulging brown paper bag. Daisy's mouth watered and she licked her lips. How wonderful to have a whole shop just for lollies. If only she could take some home for Flora.

'Come on,' Elsie said. 'You're starving, I can tell.'

'I should really be getting back . . .' said
Daisy, but she was starting to feel a little light-
headed with hunger. Pushing down her fear of
Aunty May, she followed Elsie into the crowd
as Mabel walked ahead of them.

Daisy had once looked into a kaleidoscope
and seen all the colors and shapes moving and
changing, and that's just what the city looked
like to her: a collection of vivid, bright colours,
constantly moving and changing. Then she
noticed several lines of men, their faces grey
and desperate, winding down the city streets.

'If they hear of a job going they'll queue
all day,' Elsie explained, 'but usually only one
person will get hired.'

Daisy thought of her dad. She hoped he'd
had better luck than these sad-faced men.

'Righto, this is it,' Mabel said, as they
turned the corner.

Just ahead of them Daisy could see there
was a crowded street market. Drawing closer,

a mixture of smells hit her; the tang of just-picked flowers and horse dung, wet dirt and fish mingled in her nostrils. All the fresh food reminded her of Dad's vegie garden back home. Her stomach rumbled noisily and her mouth watered. She stood mesmerised by the vibrant colors and sounds as shoppers haggled for bargains and stallholders shouted out their prices to the crowds:

'Ham hocks, get your cut-price ham hocks.'

'Lambs fry, cook it up for your man's dinner.'

'Best spuds in town, get 'em while they're fresh.'

'This is the back of the market,' Elsie told her as they finally came to a gap in the crowds. 'It's the best spot.'

'For what?' All Daisy could see was a row of bins, empty crates and a butcher's cart filled with old bones.

'We'll have to be fast,' Elsie said and ran nimbly to the bins. She rummaged around inside one. 'Ah ha,' she cried, holding up a crumpled paper bag with what looked like the leftovers of a fruit bun inside it.

Daisy watched in shock as Mabel scrabbled in the bin beside her sister, her head almost hidden inside it. Urgh. Am I hungry enough to do *that*? she wondered.

Elsie pointed to the stack of wooden crates, 'Quick, Daisy,' she said, 'check in there.'

This is ridiculous, Daisy said to herself. I don't care what that man in The Myer Emporium thought – I'm not a beggar.

But her stomach reminded her that she hadn't eaten since lunch yesterday, and who knew when Dad's money would arrive?

And then, in the corner of the very bottom crate she saw an orange. Even though its skin was a bit dark and shrivelled, Daisy could almost taste it. She reached over the pile of crates to claim it, but her arm wasn't long enough.

'Get out of there, you dirty little scabs,

before I call the coppers!' a shrill voice
screamed at them.

'Run, Daisy, run!' Elsie cried, sprinting
into the street with Mabel fast behind her.

'You grimy rat, get out of that bin,' the
voice shouted again, closer this time, and
Daisy looked up to see a large woman heading
towards her waving a cane. 'I'll teach you to
steal from me,' she yelled.

Daisy looked at the orange, then back at the
woman. Then, in a lightning-fast decision, she
pushed the top few crates off the pile, thrust
her arm down through the slats and felt the
soft flesh of the orange. She grasped it tightly
and, pulling her arm out, ran wildly away. As
she heard the woman's heavy footsteps behind
her, she realised that, like it or not, her life
really had changed forever.

4
Lost and Found

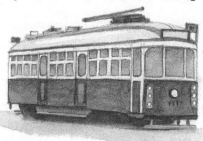

DAISY ran through narrow streets where thin children stared at her with listless, hollow eyes. They looked like ghosts. I don't care what I have to do, thought Daisy, we're not ending up like *that*. She sprinted through another stretch of green park, not stopping until she was completely out of breath and her legs wobbled. Finally she dropped to a crouch on a street corner, panting heavily, the orange a sticky mess in her hand. She peeled it quickly and held it over her head, and then let the juice drip into her mouth, savouring the sweetness.

She couldn't wait to share it with the others. When her breathing returned to normal, she stood up and looked around her. She suddenly realised that she had no idea where she was and there was no sign of Elsie and Mabel.

Daisy took a deep breath and tried to calm down but the world was spinning around her. What if she never found her way back to the house? She wasn't even supposed to have left. Who would take care of Flora?

She imagined herself after ten years of living on the street, toothless and thin, her hair matted with lice and dirt, begging for food scraps and unable to remember her own name or where she was from. Suddenly Melbourne didn't seem so marvellous after all. Tears fell down her cheeks and she threw the orange onto the footpath in frustration.

'This stupid, stupid city,' she cried aloud. This would never happen in the country, where she knew every hill and paddock, every tree and road like they were her own backyard. She longed to be home, where everything was familiar and safe.

'You're not going to waste a perfectly good orange, are you?' a voice asked.

Daisy looked up. It was Elsie, panting with exhaustion, her tangled hair plastered to her forehead with sweat. A minute later Mabel flopped beside her on the street, trying to catch her breath.

'I'll give you one thing, country girl, you sure can run fast,' Mabel said.

Daisy threw her arms around Mabel and hugged her in relief. 'I thought I'd lost you! I thought I was all alone with no idea how to get home. I thought I was going to have to live on the streets for the rest of my life!'

'Geez, you're a dramatic one, aren't you?' Mabel said with a laugh. 'Nah, we were waiting for you round the corner from the market, but then you went and ran in the opposite direction, so we followed you.'

'I reckon the orange is still good,' Elsie said, splitting it into three pieces.

The sweetness burst into Daisy's mouth like sunshine. On the farm, she and Amelia ate as much fruit as they wanted, right off the trees in summer, but this was the first fruit she'd tasted since leaving home.

'Let's finish the rest of the food in the park,' Mabel suggested, dragging Daisy to her feet.

The friends walked slowly back to the park on their tired legs.

'This is a good spot,' Mabel said, leading them to a large stone bandstand under a group of trees. 'We can have a picnic in here.'

Mabel and Elsie emptied their pockets onto the ground. There was half a fruit bun, a bruised apple and a hard piece of cheese.

'It's a feast!' Elsie tore the bun into equal pieces. 'Go on.'

Daisy gazed at her share hungrily, but she

knew she shouldn't stay. 'I have to go.'

'Don't worry, Daisy,' said Mabel. 'Let's eat up quick and then we'll get you back – we know the quick way home.'

'What's the quick way?'

'We're going to hop a tram.'

'What?' Daisy asked, chewing her lip with alarm.

'It's really easy, just watch what we do, and hold on tight,' Mabel said.

'But how . . . .' Daisy began.

'Trams have doors on both sides,' Elsie interrupted her. 'They only use one side, depending which way they're going. So we hop on the steps on the other side, hold onto the pole, and get a free ride.' She gave Daisy a confident grin as they wolfed down their spoils. 'Just don't try to get off until we're stopped. A boy lost his foot under the tram that way last week.'

Daisy wasn't sure it sounded like a good idea, but when they'd finished eating she followed the twins as they ran to a tram stop in the middle of the busy road.

She was full of nerves as the yellow-and-green tram drew closer. Finally it shuddered to a stop and passengers clambered out while others waited to get on board. She darted around to the other side of the tram with the twins and watched as they climbed on the steps. They looked so high.

'Come on, Daisy, you'll be fine,' Elsie called.

The tram was getting ready to move again so Daisy quickly jumped up between Mabel and Elsie and held on tight to the pole beside the steps.

'Here we go,' Mabel called as the tram lurched forward on its tracks and began trundling down the street.

'Oh my goodness, oh my goodness,' Daisy cried, the wind rushing into her face, streaming her hair behind her. As the tram clattered through intersections and around corners, passing cars and pedestrians on either side, it almost felt as if she was galloping through the fields with Jimmy again. For the first time since coming to the city, with food in her belly and friends by her side, Daisy felt light and free. She tilted her head back and closed her eyes. I might be poor, she thought, but I'm the hero in this story, and it's time to take things into my own hands.

When the tram reached a stop, the twins bobbed their heads beneath the window to hide from the ticket inspector. Daisy joined them and the three girls crouched in a row, shaking with excited laughter. The tram soon ground to halt and they jumped down from the steps and snuck behind it and onto the footpath.

'That was *so* much fun.' Daisy sighed happily. 'Thanks for the adventure.'

'Glad you liked it.' Elsie beamed. 'Will we be seeing you round again, then?'

'Absolutely. Unless . . . Well . . .'

'Well, spit it out,' said Mabel.

'How do I get a job?' asked Daisy. 'I mean, where do I look?'

'They tape up signs at the newsagents every morning,' said Mabel. 'You've got to get there early, though, if you want a chance.'

'And you're probably too small,' added Elsie. 'But good luck. Hope your aunty's not too mad that you were gone so long.'

'Oh geez,' Daisy said, remembering. 'Thanks.' She took a deep breath, opened the back door, and stepped into the cold kitchen, careful not to let it slam behind her.

'Oh, so you've decided to sneak back in, have you?' Aunty May said. She was sitting at the kitchen table, combing Flora's hair.

'Hi, Daisy,' Flora called. 'Aunty May is braiding my hair. Don't you think it's lovely?'

Daisy's stomach churned. '*I* always braid your hair for you, Flossy,' she said.

'Well, you weren't here, were you?' Aunty

May said. 'You were out gallivanting around the streets.' Her small mouth pursed with anger. 'After I *expressly* forbade you to leave the house.' She put down the brush and glared at Daisy. 'I can see I will have to keep a tighter rein on you, my girl.'

Daisy flushed with embarrassment. She wasn't a baby who needed to be supervised, for goodness sake, but she didn't want to say anything that would make Aunty May even angrier. She swallowed. 'I was perfectly safe.'

'Well, then, if you're so clever at getting around the city, you can get yourself a job right away,' Aunty May said.

'I'd already decided I would,' Daisy snapped back.

'Don't get snitchy with me,' her aunt answered. 'And if you're not bringing money into this house within the next month . . .' she glowered at Daisy, 'well, let's just say I'll only be able to afford to feed *one* extra mouth.'

5
Blood and Guts

Two weeks later, the clip-clop of the milkman's horse woke Daisy before dawn. She lay snuggled beside Flora, listening to the low rumble of the cart rolling down the laneway and the clink of bottles being placed in doorways.

And there's the night carter, she thought as she heard the now-familiar scrape of the dunny can being dragged from the outhouse and replaced with a clean one.

The jagged crow of a rooster somewhere down the laneway told her it was time to get up.

If I could just get my arm free, she thought, trying to slide her numb arm from beneath Flora's heavy head. She heard her sister's tummy rumble loudly beside her.

'I'll get work today, I promise, Flossy,' Daisy whispered. 'Then I'll buy us a proper dinner.' She stroked her sister's thin face. 'Now go back to sleep.'

'I love ya, Daisy,' Flora mumbled.

'I love ya too, Flossy.'

Daisy shook her arm to get rid of the pins-and-needles, and dressed quickly. She dragged her boots on at the front door and was outside within minutes.

Fog hovered across the laneway, softening the edges of the world and leaving shimmering dew drops on the few spring bulbs that had forced through the bricks to bloom yellow and pink in the early spring sunshine.

It almost looks pretty, Daisy thought, shivering with cold as she hurried up the lane.

She was happy to find she was one of the first at the newsagent this morning. Daisy had been coming every morning, so far with no luck. And worse yet, Amelia's letters kept coming but there had still been nothing from Dad, and Aunty May was getting meaner by the day.

Why hadn't Dad written? Could he have broken his leg somewhere on the track and be lying there, injured? Maybe he'd been kidnapped? Or murdered by bushrangers? Daisy's mind jumped from thought to thought as she scanned the job ads taped up on the newsagent's window.

The gut factory needed several workers. The twins had told her about the factory, where gut was cut out of dead animals, washed and then made into things like tennis racket strings and sausage skin. It sounded disgusting, but Daisy was desperate. The thought of leaving Flora and being thrown out on the streets to starve was too awful to contemplate.

The factory is just a few minutes away. I can easily be one of the first in the queue, she thought. I'm going to get work today – I know I am, she decided as she ran in the direction of the factory. Then I'm going to buy some food for Flora so she doesn't look so pale and sick all the time.

There were just a few women at the front door of the factory and Daisy hurried to join the queue. By the time the foreman opened the door, the line stretched halfway down the street.

'Right, we need eight women today, so I'll take the first in the queue,' he said. There was a groan from the crowd and the women at the back began to melt away.

As he pointed at the front of the line, Daisy quickly counted heads. That's me, that's me, I'm number eight! she thought excitedly, hopping from foot to foot to keep warm.

She stood as tall as she could as the women in front of her started to move into the factory.

'They'll never take you,' the woman behind her sneered. 'You're just a titch of a thing. They wouldn't get their bob's worth out of you.'

'I can work just as hard as anyone,' Daisy replied, frowning.

'What have we here, then?' the foreman laughed as Daisy reached the front door. 'You're not going to do me much good, little sprat,' he said, patting Daisy's head.

She squirmed away. 'I'm small but I can work hard, and I really need the work, Mister. I want to bring my dad home from the bush and buy my sister something proper to eat.'

'Forget her,' the woman behind her said, roughly pushing Daisy aside. 'I'm your eighth worker today, Joe. I was here last week, and I got a whole family of kids with empty bellies.'

'*Please?*' Daisy said, staring up at the foreman, twisting her hands in front of her.

'Trouble is, little'un, you wouldn't even reach the benches in here,' he said. He nodded at the woman behind Daisy and she marched triumphantly into the factory.

Daisy bowed her head and turned to leave.

'I tell you what,' Joe said, spitting on the ground in front of him. 'I'll give you sixpence if you wanna muck out the gut buckets.'

'Yes, sir!' Sixpence would pay for dinner at least.

'Righto.' Joe jerked his thumb in the direction of the factory and Daisy ran to follow him inside.

A solid wall of stench hit her as soon as she entered the dim building. She gagged and covered her face with her hands in horror as the smell of rotted animal guts flooded her nostrils. It was like being inside a dead sheep.

Joe laughed. 'The first few minutes are the worst,' he said. 'You'll get used to it soon enough.' He slapped Daisy on the back and she fought the urge to vomit.

'Now, the slops buckets are at the end of each of the benches. There's a dozen benches. You need to drag the buckets to the trench out the back and chuck 'em in, then put the buckets back where they were.'

He pointed to the back door of the factory. 'The trench is out there. Shouldn't take you more than a few hours. Off you go.'

With that he strode away, leaving Daisy still trying to breathe properly in the thick air.

All around her men stood cleaning lengths of grisly animal intestine, cutting off the flecks of red flesh and leaving white lengths of skin that Daisy guessed must be the gut. The men threw the meat scraps into buckets at the end of the benches.

Oh those poor, poor animals, she thought. I can't do this. It's so cruel!

The dreadful stench wound itself into her mouth and choked the back of her throat, making her splutter and cough.

She noticed the women who had been hired this morning washing the long stretches of gut in the far corner of the factory, and she wanted to throw up all over again.

It's for Flora. It's to keep us off the streets, she reminded herself, trying to swallow the awful feeling in her throat. She pulled her hair back from her face, wound it on top of her head in a bun, and made her way to the first bench, where the slops bucket was overflowing with discarded intestine.

She took a deep breath and grabbed the handles of the bucket, trying to keep it as far away from her as possible as she dragged it along the filthy wooden floor.

The bucket was heavy and awkward to move. Daisy felt her arms and shoulders aching with every step. She tripped more than once on the uneven floorboards and had to go slowly in case she tipped the bucket over.

I'd rather *die* than have to clean this muck off the floor with my bare hands, she thought with disgust.

Finally she reached the back door and stepped gratefully into the fresh air. She fought to pull the heavy bucket onto its side, grunting with effort as she struggled to tip it into a deep trench that buzzed with black blowflies.

With a final determined push, she watched as the collection of gruesome scraps slopped into the trench. Take that!

She gagged again and had to walk away from the trench, gulping mouthfuls of fresh air to stop herself from being sick.

Her head was throbbing and her face streamed with sweat. And that's just one bucket, she thought in desperation. How can I do eleven more?

Daisy leant against the back wall to catch her breath. She could just leave now and no one would ever know, she realised. But then she remembered how thin and pale Flora looked these days. She thought about the ghost children she'd seen in the city, and grimly picked up the bucket and went back into the putrid air of the factory, her head buzzing.

This is all Dad's fault, Daisy thought, gritting her teeth. He should have written! He should be taking care of us, not forcing me to work in this disgusting factory. I should be at school with Amelia, with Jimmy tied up outside waiting for me.

In her last letter Amelia had told Daisy that she'd finished writing the play with another friend, Lucy Bell, and they had performed it in Amelia's front room with Lucy playing Daisy's part. Daisy's heart hurt so much when she thought about this, she could hardly bear it. Someone else playing her part, in her play, and here she was wrestling with animal guts just so she could feed her sister. As she emptied each disgusting bucket, the salty taste of tears grew stronger on her tongue.

Four hours later she had replaced the final bucket back in its spot and went to look for Joe. 'I'm all done,' she said, barely able to speak with exhaustion.

'Good on ya, kid,' Joe said, reaching into his pocket, 'You won me a coupla bob.' He handed her six pennies.

'What do you mean?' Daisy asked, brightening up when she saw the money.

'A coupla blokes bet me you couldn't do the job, but I reckoned you could, so now I can collect me winnings.' He threw his head back with laughter and Daisy saw the rotten stumps of his teeth.

'You hired me just for a bet?'

'Well, not just a bet – you got your cash, didn't you?' He reached over to tousle Daisy's hair with his calloused hand. 'But no more lining up for work, you hear? Grow a bit first.' He gave another chuckle and walked away.

Daisy went to sit in the weak sunlight outside the factory. She closed her eyes and let her tired head drop as she thought about her dad again. She knew he would never really abandon them. Had he found a job yet, or was he finding it as tough as she was?

'I just hope he's okay,' she whispered to herself.

She looked at the coins in her blood-stained hand. Right, the first thing I'm going to do is wash this muck off me, then I'm going shopping, she decided.

An hour later she burst through the door of the cottage, calling for Flora. 'I told you I'd bring dinner, Flossy!' She triumphantly put a meat pie on the table as Flora came running toward her, eyes shining. Suddenly Flora stopped and looked at Daisy with horror.

'What's that awful stink?' she cried.

6
A Safe Bet

'**D**AISY? Daisy?' Aunty May's sharp voice echoed up the laneway.

Daisy stopped in the middle of the hopscotch game she was playing with Mabel and Elsie. There'd been no jobs again that morning, and she'd finished her chores for the day – or so she'd thought.

'I'd better be off,' Daisy said. 'My stone's on the three, though. No cheating, you two.'

'Who us?' Elsie said innocently.

'We'd never do that,' continued Mabel with a giggle.

'Hmm, a likely story,' Daisy said, and turned to run back to the house.

Maybe a letter's finally come from Dad! she thought. Oh please, please let that be it. A lovely long letter, and money for food so she'll forget about sending me away.

'There you are. Goodness knows I can never find you when I want you.' Aunty May sighed.

Daisy started to speak, but Aunty May waved a hand at her impatiently.

'I don't need your back chat. At least we might make a difference with young Flora, but with you,' she shook her head, 'there's no hope.'

No letter, then, Daisy thought sadly. She stared at her aunt's small, mean mouth as the woman continued with her list of complaints. She's just like a wicked witch in a fairytale, Daisy thought. She's probably been putting spells on us in our sleep. That's how she's got

Flossy to like her. Daisy couldn't explain it, but Flora didn't seem to mind Aunty May. *Perhaps I didn't take good enough care of her after all,* thought Daisy.

'Are you listening to a word I'm saying?'

'Yes, Aunty May,' Daisy said, and forced herself to pay attention.

'I said I'm off to clean for the Coopers, which means I won't be able to get into town for bread. That blasted baker has missed us again. I'm sure he does it on purpose.'

He misses us because we never pay the bill, Daisy thought.

'Now, here's a shilling. I don't know what I'm doing trusting you with it, but there you go.' She pointed a bony finger in Daisy's face. 'A loaf of bread costs four pence, so I want eight pence change, do you understand me?

'Maybe I should get our Flora to hold the money,' the woman muttered to herself. 'She seems to have better sense than this one . . .'

she trailed off.

'I'll be fine, Aunty May,' Daisy said, pulling her hair back from her face and twisting it in frustration. 'Flora's too young to look after the money.'

'Hmph, she may be young, but she has a better head on her shoulders than you, my dear. I've a good mind to take her in hand myself, and give her a proper upbringing before she's ruined.'

Daisy had to clamp her mouth shut to keep herself from shouting something rude.

'And stop fiddling with your hair for goodness sake, girl. No wonder it's always such a mess.' She scowled at Daisy and shook her head. 'Right, your uncle is asleep, so mind you don't wake him. I'll be back by tea time, and I want a loaf of bread and eight pence on the table, or there will be trouble. Goodness knows you're already on borrowed time here. What's it been now, six weeks? And not a single penny? Your father must think I'm a fool.'

With that she rammed her hair comb tighter in her severe bun, straightened her shabby jacket and stepped out into the lane, her shoes slapping angrily against the cobblestones.

Daisy looked down at the shiny shilling in her palm. I could buy a feast with this, she thought, and her stomach clenched with hunger. But then what?

'Aunty May'd have us living in a shanty town quick smart, that's what,' she muttered.

'Oh no Mabel, she's gone completely loopy now,' Elsie cried from behind her.

'Talking to herself, my goodness, it's not a good sign at all,' Mabel added as the twins strolled up to Daisy, arm-in-arm.

'Oh stop it,' Daisy laughed. 'I was just thinking about what would happen if I spent Aunty May's money on a big feast for all of us.'

'She'd have you living down in Dudley

Flats with all the other down-and-outers in a flash,' Mabel said.

'Yep, it would be a humpy in the mud for you in no time,' Elsie added with a wink. 'Though our ma reckons your aunty has plans for Flossy.'

Daisy felt her heart sink. 'What do you mean?' she asked.

'Well, I heard her tell our pa that old May's pretty keen to get rich, keep Flossy, stick her in some posh school and bring her up as her own kid,' Elsie said.

'Yeah, she seems to like Flossy,' Mabel added, patting Daisy's shoulder. 'But she's just rotten to you.'

Daisy crossed her arms and tossed her head. 'Well, I don't care what she thinks, there's no way she can split me and Flora up. We're family.'

'Good on ya, Daisy, you'll show her,' Elsie cried. 'Mean old cow that she is.'

Daisy giggled in spite of herself. 'Shhh, Uncle Bertie's home today. I'd hate for him to hear.'

'Well, he should stand up for you more against the old hag then,' Elsie said. 'It's just cruel how she treats you.'

'We're luckier than most people,' Daisy said. 'At least we have a roof over our heads.' For now, she added silently to herself. 'Anyway, it will all be fine once Dad sends some money. I'm sure it won't be long before a letter gets through.'

'Well, I hope he hurries up with it for your sake,' Mabel said. 'But we'd better head off now, we're working the afternoon shift today. Come on, Els.'

'Ooh lovely, another day at the pickle factory. I can't wait,' Elsie sighed, 'and I only just got the smell of vinegar off me from the last shift.' She pulled her hair over her face and gave a theatrical sniff.

'You two should be on the stage,' Daisy said as Mabel began sniffing loudly at Elsie's hair as well.

Daisy thought again about someone else playing her part in her play, and felt so overwhelmed with homesickness she couldn't breathe. She felt like the world was spinning too fast all of a sudden.

'Hey there, are you all right?' Mabel asked. 'You've gone all white.'

'Don't mind us, we act like a pair of gooses sometimes,' Elsie said.

Daisy smiled weakly. 'Geese,' she said, looking up at the twins.

'What?'

'Not gooses, geese.'

'Oh well, have it your way, country girl. I expect you're the expert on bird life.'

Daisy took a shuddering breath and felt the wave of sadness lift as she looked at her two new friends, who were still staring quizzically.

'Oh, go on then.' She flapped her hands at them. 'Off to the pickle factory with you.'

'You sure you're all right?' Mabel asked over her shoulder as the twins headed up the lane.

'I'll be fine.' Daisy smiled.

She went into the dim house and found Flora lying face-down on the kitchen floor staring through the cracks in the timber to the ground underneath.

'What on earth are you doing?' Daisy asked.

'I miss Barnaby and Jess, and the chooks,' Flora said, and pushed her face even closer to the splintered floorboards. 'I'm trying to make friends with the rats so I can have a pet here.'

'Get up, you dill,' Daisy said with a laugh. 'I miss the animals too, but I don't reckon rats would be much fun to play with.'

Flora sighed. 'Bye bye, ratties,' she said and pulled herself up from the floor. 'Daisy,' she said, picking up Bunny and chewing on his ear, 'why hasn't Daddy written to us? Doesn't he love us anymore? That's what Aunty May says. Aunty May knows lots of things.'

Daisy's stomach lurched sickeningly. She rushed to hug her sister. 'Of course he loves us, Flossy. Don't ever doubt that. Daddy would never, ever let us down.' Daisy rubbed her nose with the back of her hand to try to stop her own tears.

'I'm sure he must have a very good reason why he hasn't written. Or maybe he has written; maybe lots and lots of letters, but they got lost somehow.'

'But Daisy, it's been so long now, and Aunty May is getting ever so cross with you, and I'm always so hungry. What will we do if a letter never comes?'

'Flossy, listen to me. Our dad will take care of us, no matter what. It might be taking a long time, but we can't give up on him yet.

He would never give up on us.' Daisy hugged her sister even tighter, then reached down to tickle her stomach. 'Remember how Daddy always did this?'

Flora burst into laughter and squirmed out of Daisy's reach, falling on to the floor with an excited squeal.

'What do we have here?' Uncle Bertie asked as he came out of his bedroom scratching his belly beneath his undershirt.

'Oh no, I'm so sorry, Uncle Bertie, did we wake you?' Daisy quickly pulled Flora to her feet.

'Now, now, don't go getting yourself all flustered,' Uncle Bertie said. 'I was about ready to wake up anyway, a man can't sleep the afternoon away, even if it is his day off.' He gave Daisy a cheery wink, then noticed the shilling coin sitting on the table.

'Someone's in the money,' he said, his eyes lighting up.

'I wish I was,' Daisy said. 'But it's Aunty May's money. I'm to get a loaf of bread for her.'

'Aah, I see, she's trusting the urchin with the money now is she?'

Daisy's face flushed with anger at the word, but her uncle roared with laughter.

'I'm just havin' a lend of you, girl. Come on, we'll make an afternoon stroll of it, shall we? Just give me a sec to get my shirt on.'

Within minutes, Daisy, Flora and Uncle Bertie were on their way up the lane, the girls holding hands and Uncle Bertie whistling a merry tune, and the world didn't seem so bad after all.

'Lovely afternoon, Mrs Roberts,' Uncle Bertie called, dipping his hat to Mabel and Elsie's mum, who was hanging washing on a rope line. 'You're looking a picture as always.'

'That's enough of you with your silver tongue, Mr Sanderson,' Mrs Roberts retorted and gave the girls a quick smile.

'What, me? The picture of decency, aren't I?' Uncle Bertie protested. 'Taking my lovely nieces for a stroll on a pleasant afternoon.'

Flora giggled and skipped ahead.

'Wait for us at the corner,' Daisy called. 'The road's too busy for you to cross alone.'

'Ah, she's all right, we don't need to cross here,' Uncle Bertie said.

'But the bakery is that way.' Daisy pointed across the road.

'You're right there, me girl, but what say I take us on a little adventure first?' he suggested as they caught up to Flora.

'Somewhere fun?' Flora asked, clapping her hands with excitement.

'Oh my word, yes,' he replied.

Daisy bit her lip with worry. 'Will we still get to the bakery before it closes?'

'No doubt about it.'

'Is your detour far?' she asked.

'It's just at the end of this next lane,' he said,

rushing the girls along the street.

What could it be? Daisy wondered. Pictures of Queenie the elephant flitted into her head. Could it be the zoo? Maybe they'd get to have a ride on Queenie and to see the lions and the monkeys. Delicious excitement bubbled inside her. It was a strange feeling after the weeks of worry.

'Here we go, my lovelies,' said Uncle Bertie as he steered them into a tiny alleyway.

Oh. Daisy's excitement drained away. It's just a stupid alleyway.

A man standing on the corner of the alley gave Uncle Bertie a quick nod as they walked past. 'Big group today,' he said.

'You beauty,' Uncle Bertie replied, and quickened his pace.

A big group of what? Daisy wondered. She looked back at the man curiously. 'Who is that man waiting for?'

'Oh, he's just the cockatoo, love. It's his job

to keep a look out for the ah . . . well, just a
look out.'

Daisy was confused. She fiddled with her
hair uneasily, and grabbed Flora's hand tighter.
Something didn't quite feel right.

She noticed there was a group of men
standing in a circle ahead of them. A cloud of
cigarette smoke swirled above their heads and
loud bursts of laughter and excited shouting
echoed up the lane.

Uncle Bertie stopped and crouched in front
of Daisy and Flora. He pushed his hat back
on his head and Daisy could see his neatly
combed grey hair. He gave them a big smile
and reached out to pull Daisy in closer.

'Now, how would you girls feel about a spot
of ice cream?' he asked.

'Ooh, yes please,' Flora cried with delight.

Daisy's mouth watered. Ice cream! Maybe
the afternoon *would* turn out well. 'We'd love
that, Uncle Bertie.'

'Alrighty then, here's the plan,' he said, giving the girls a big wink. 'You give me a quick borrow of that lovely shilling coin you've got there, and when I'm finished having a bit of a muck around with me mates, we'll all go and get ice cream.'

Daisy took a step back, her fingers tightening around the coin. Aunty May would fry her alive if she didn't come home with a loaf of bread and eight pence change.

'We can't, Uncle Bertie. Aunty May will be so cross . . .'

'Don't you worry your head about May,' he interrupted. 'She'll never know a thing. I'm going to invest that little shilling in a special game here called Two Up. Now, I'm a bit of an expert in these parts, so I'll quickly turn that shilling into ice-cream money, and maybe even dinner besides.'

'Oh, please Daisy,' Flora implored. 'We could even have ice cream for dinner.'

Daisy turned the coin over and over in her fingers. Should she give him the coin? Wasn't it his money, too? And if he was so good at this game then surely it would be all right?

'But we still have to remember the bread, Uncle Bertie, no matter how much ice cream we eat.'

Uncle Bertie gave a whoop of delight, grabbed the coin from Daisy's outstretched hand and ran to join the circle of men.

'Come on, you blokes, make room, make room,' he said, pushing into the circle.

Daisy and Flora walked closer to watch the game. I hope I made the right decision, Daisy thought, her heart pounding.

A man in the middle of the circle put two pennies on the end of a small piece of wood, then flipped them into the air. Daisy noticed how carefully the men watched, tilting their heads to the sky as the pennies spun in space, then tracing their journey back down again.

When the coins hit the ground there was silence for a second as each man leaned in to take a look, then the group erupted into a mix of cheers and groans. One man with a bushy black beard pulled his cap down over his forehead, stuck his hands in his pockets and walked dejectedly away, while others slapped a tall, skinny player on the back.

'Look at all the money,' Flora gasped, pointing at a man with a wad of notes in his hand and a cigarette hanging from the corner of his mouth. He was rapidly passing out cash and being handed notes and coins, all the while calling out numbers and names, and squinting through the haze of cigarette smoke.

When the crowd around him cleared, he counted up all the notes and nodded at Uncle Bertie. 'Come in, spinner,' he said.

Uncle Bertie pushed to the middle of the circle and took his turn to flip the coins into the air.

There were more cries of excitement and disappointment as the coins landed near his feet. Money was frantically swapped once more, and the process started again.

Is that all they do? Daisy wondered. It doesn't seem nearly as much fun as hopscotch.

Uncle Bertie played game after game as more men wandered down the lane to join in and others peeled off as their money ran out.

Is he ever going to finish? Daisy thought after more than an hour of watching. The bakery would be shutting soon.

Flora gave a loud yawn. 'Can't we go yet?' she whined.

Suddenly a high-pitched whistle echoed up the alley. It was the cockatoo. 'Cops,' he shouted urgently, bolting from the lane.

Chaos broke out, men grabbed for their money, spat their cigarettes to the ground and fled in all directions.

'Run, girls!' Uncle Bertie shouted. 'Forget

the money!' He turned and sprinted away, his pinned-up jacket sleeve flapping behind him.

Daisy didn't have time to think. 'Quick, in here, Flossy,' she cried, pulling Flora into a small hole in a fence behind them. Daisy could hear the heavy tramp of boots on the cobbled laneway as policemen stormed past their hiding spot.

'What's happening, Daisy?' Flora's voice trembled with fear. 'Will we be sent to prison?'

'Of course not, Floss. Come on, this way,' Daisy urged, pushing her through the small yard they were in. Soon they were in another lane, flanked on both sides by half-empty shops with dirty windows with only one or two faded items.

I can't believe Uncle Bertie would leave us like that! Daisy thought, her face hot with anger, as they stopped to catch their breath.

Then a much worse thought hit her. Aunty May's money! They had no bread, and no money, and something told her Uncle Bertie wouldn't tell Aunty May the truth.

She felt sick with fear. We're on our own, she realised. I'll have to fix this, and fast.

'Oh no,' Flora groaned, 'Uncle Bertie lost all the money. What will we do?'

Daisy could see that Flora was shaking. Daisy wanted to run. To run and run until she got back to the farm and Jimmy, the cats and all the animals. She wanted to run in the kitchen door and see Dad sitting at the table and have everything back to normal. Back to when Amelia was right next door, and their stomachs were full and a maths test seemed like the worst thing that could happen.

She sat on the cold ground, with her back against a sagging fence, pulled her knees up and wrapped her arms around them, then lay her head on her arms and sobbed.

7
A Great Idea

'**P**LEASE don't cry,' Flora whispered, creeping up to sit beside her big sister. She rubbed Daisy's arm. 'It will be okay.'

Daisy took a deep breath, sniffed loudly a few times, and put her head up to look at Flora, who gave her a weak smile.

'You always think of something, Daisy,' Flora said. 'Like when you're making up one of your plays, you always think of such good ideas.' She snuggled in closer.

Daisy nodded, and sniffed again. 'All right then, Floss, if this was a play, what would I do next, do you think? The heroines have lost their treasure and the evil witch is going to boil them up in her cauldron if they go home without it. What can they do?'

Flora giggled. 'Maybe they could take the witch some flowers?' she suggested. 'Or maybe they could use a magic spell to make more money.'

'Well, that would be handy,' Daisy said, 'if only we knew *that* spell we could . . .' She stopped, her eyes suddenly shining with excitement. 'Flowers!' she exclaimed, jumping to her feet. 'Flora, you're brilliant. Come on!'

'What are we doing here?' Flora asked, puffing for breath, as they ran into the Fitzroy Gardens ten minutes later.

'I remembered that Mabel and Elsie told me they pick flowers here sometimes,' Daisy said.

'Maybe we can make some bunches, then go to the posh part of the city and sell them.'

Flora smiled. 'I love flowers.'

I just hope it works, Daisy thought, because it's the only plan I have.

They found a garden bed where early spring blooms were bursting from the ground.

'This purple one is so pretty,' Flora said, 'and it smells so nice.'

'And look, there's lots of freesias,' Daisy pointed out a patch of small multicolored flowers. 'Remember we used to pick these back at the farm?'

The girls quickly gathered enough flowers to make twelve small bunches.

'Now, we'll use this to tie them up,' Daisy said, pulling off her jacket and starting to pick at the seam.

'But you'll be cold,' Flora protested.

'It's getting warmer now,' Daisy said. 'I'll be fine.' She tore a strip off, and quickly tied it into a bow around several of the flowers to make a pretty bunch.

Flora helped by separating the remaining blooms into equal groups.

'Hey! What are you girls doing in my garden?' boomed an angry voice. 'Wait till I get my hands on you!'

Oh no, that's the gardener! Daisy thought, as a crooked little man in dirty overalls stomped toward them. 'Run, Flora!' Daisy cried and they sprinted out as fast as they could.

They ducked into a bus stop to hide, then kept on towards the smarter streets where the rich people did their shopping. Why was everyone in the city so grumpy all the time? Daisy thought. Back home you could pick flowers anywhere and no one ever minded.

'Now we'll stand on this corner together,' Daisy said, finding a sunny spot near some expensive shops, 'and see if we can sell these.'

Daisy gave Flora half the flowers, took half

herself and, planting a bright smile on her face, began approaching the passing shoppers.

'Flowers, Madam, pretty flowers for your table. Just a penny.'

'Spring flowers, sir, perfect for your wife. Only a penny a bunch.'

The shoppers simply walked on past, tightening their wool overcoats and fancy furs as if they might catch something nasty from the scruffy girls.

After an hour, Flora gave up and sat on the cold footpath, her head on her knees.

Daisy felt so embarrassed, like a beggar desperate for money. But what choice did she have? If they went home without the bread and money, Aunty May would throw them out onto the street for sure. She tried to ignore the angry looks and haughty frowns of the rich ladies who shooed her away as if she was an annoying blowfly. But as each one pushed past her, she burned with shame. Please,

please, someone just stop and buy one bunch, she thought as she rubbed at the goose bumps that covered her bare arms.

The sun got lower in the sky, the sounds of the traffic grew louder and trams trundled past noisily. Still Daisy stood on her corner calling out to the passing shoppers.

The flowers are going to wilt soon, then we'll have no hope, Daisy thought. We won't even bother going back to Aunty May's. I'll have to find us somewhere else to sleep, maybe in the park. She stomped on the spot to shake the pins and needles from her feet.

She heard Flora sobbing quietly with cold and tiredness, and was almost ready to give in when a lady in a stylish red coat approached.

'Would you like some flowers, Madam?' Daisy asked weakly.

'Well, if it isn't the little girl who saved my Oscar.'

Daisy looked closely at the woman and

realised with a shock that it was Mrs Johnson from the train all those weeks ago. I can't believe I imagined Aunty May might be like her, Daisy thought sadly.

'You were so brave that day, my dear. Did your aunt buy you a nice treat as a reward?' Mrs Johnson asked.

Daisy opened her mouth to answer, but all that came out was a croak, and before she knew it fat tears were rolling down her face, making a trail on her dirty cheeks.

'Oh my poor girl, whatever's the matter?' Mrs Johnson put a gloved hand on Daisy's arm.

'It was the shilling,' Daisy sobbed, her words coming out in sharp gasps. 'Uncle Bertie threw the money in the air. He said we'd have an ice cream, then the police came and now there's no bread and we'll have to live in a shanty town.' She buried her face in her hands and sobbed for the second time that day. At the sight of Daisy's tears, Flora jumped up, threw her small arms around Daisy's waist and cried into her dress.

Mrs Johnson took out a lace-hemmed handkerchief from her purse. 'There, there,' she soothed, and passed Daisy the hanky. 'Let's just step back a bit off the corner, so we're not in everyone's way.' She gently steered Daisy onto a bench. 'Now take a deep breath, dear, and try to explain again.'

Daisy gently wiped the corners of her eyes with the pretty material, trying not to get it dirty. 'Thank you,' she said, handing it back. She breathed deeply and explained about their awful day.

'I see,' said Mrs Johnson, nodding her head thoughtfully when Daisy was finished. 'Well, that's rather lucky for me, actually. You see I'm having some guests over for dinner tonight, and what I really need are some spring flowers to brighten the table.'

Daisy looked at her, her eyes widening with hope.

'So let me see, how many bunches do you have? And they're a penny each? Perfect, I'll take them all. Here you are,' she said, and fished in her purse for a coin. 'One shilling.'

She's the kindest person I ever met, Daisy thought, as a thick fog of worry lifted off her. I'll bet she doesn't even need flowers – she's just helping us out.

'Now I must get on with my shopping, and I believe you have an important errand to run?' She touched Daisy's cheek. 'Remember how strong and brave you are, dear,' she said, then waved goodbye as she walked away.

'Does this mean everything is all right?' Flora asked, turning her freckled face up to look at Daisy.

'Everything is wonderful, Flossy,' Daisy replied, feeling lighter and happier than she had all day. 'Now let's go and get that bread.'

8
Tempers Flare

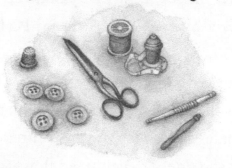

'**H**AVE you finished that darning yet, girl?'

'I'm on the last sock, Aunty May,' Daisy answered. She straightened her aching back, and rubbed her hands together for warmth. I must've darned a million socks in the past two weeks, Daisy thought. I may as well be a slave.

Life at Aunty May's had gotten worse in the past fortnight. Uncle Bertie had stopped making jokes since the Two Up game. Maybe he's worried I'll tell Aunty May what happened, Daisy thought. But I wouldn't do that – she'd only find a way to blame me for it.

'Stop dawdling, for goodness sake,' Aunty May snapped, looking over the top of her teacup. 'It has to be delivered before dark. You can't expect to freeload here, you know, not with your dad doing a runner.'

Daisy was so tired and stiff from sewing for the past few hours that she didn't have the energy to answer. She had tried so hard to be good and hold her tongue, but today it all felt too much. A tear dribbled slowly down Daisy's cheek. Where was Dad? Didn't he care – even a little bit?

She'd gone over this hundreds of times before. Maybe he had forgotten the address. Maybe he had no money to buy stamps. Maybe he'd got sick and couldn't write. She shook the thought from her head angrily and kicked the table leg in frustration.

'Stop that,' Aunty May scolded.

'Sorry, Aunty May,' she sighed. She tied a knot in the cotton and threw the sock onto a large pile beside her.

'Flora,' Aunty May yelled out the back door, 'come and get the basket. Mrs O'Halloran wants it by five o'clock.'

'Yi Le is going to help me,' Flora said as she and her friend ran in to pick up the basket of mending. 'We'll be back soon.'

'Mind you get the money, dear, and ask Mrs O'Halloran where her Rose goes to school. We might need to enrol you there soon.'

Flora smiled as she and Yi Le manoeuvred themselves and the basket out the back door.

'You ending up here might just be a blessing for poor little Flora,' said Aunty May.

Daisy felt a stab of anger, and then of jealousy. She didn't know if Aunty May was doing it to spite her, but she had been awfully friendly to Flora lately, and had even made her a new dress this week. Daisy felt more alone than ever. She stood up and arched her back with a groan. I feel like I'm about a hundred years old, she thought. I wonder if my hair's gone grey already.

'No point in moaning and carrying on, girl. If I hadn't found that mending work for you, you'd be in a pretty pickle all right,' Aunty May said, as she stirred a mutton stew on the stove. 'Not a penny from that father of yours, and not a single word for months.'

'It's only been weeks, Aunty May,' Daisy corrected her, 'and I was thinking I might go to the post office and see if his letters haven't been getting through. Maybe he has the wrong address.'

'Wrong address my foot,' her aunt scoffed. She came toward Daisy waving the wooden spoon menacingly. 'He planned it from the start, that cowardly no-hoper, dump his kids on us and make off for the bush as fast as his legs could carry him.'

'No!' cried Daisy. 'You're wrong! Dad loves

us, and he'd never, ever desert us. And Flora is *my* family, not yours.'

'You?' Aunty May spat. 'What good are you to her? What that girl needs is a mother, and I'm just the person for the job.'

Daisy was shaking with anger. She stamped her foot. 'I hate you!'

Aunty May flew across the room to land a sharp slap on Daisy's cheek. 'That's it, I've had it with you, girl,' Aunty May screamed. 'Get your things and get out!'

Daisy put a hand to her burning cheek, her thoughts racing with fear. Her face stung and she looked at her aunt with shock. 'But it's almost night time. Where will I go?'

'Go and live in the gutter for all I care.'

Daisy stumbled blindly to the little room she and Flora shared. She grabbed her photo of Jimmy, the lock of his mane and Amelia's letters. She had nothing else to take. She was shaking all over and could hardly see through her tears. 'I won't go without my sister,' she said when she returned to the kitchen with her few possessions.

'You'd rather see her live on the street too, would you? Than be fed and looked after?' Aunty May gave her an icy look and folded her arms across her chest.

She was right. At least here Flora would get food and shelter. Who knew what would happen to them on the streets?

'Right then.' Aunty May flung open the front door of the cottage and stood back waiting for Daisy to leave.

'Fine, you old crow,' Daisy cried. 'I'd rather live in a rubbish dump than here with you anyway.' She stomped out the door, then turned back. 'And don't think you've got away with this – I'll be back with my dad for Flossy. We won't let you take her.'

Aunty May slammed the door in her face, and suddenly Daisy was on the street and alone.

HOW I BECAME AN AUSTRALIAN GIRL

Michelle Hamer

I was born in a hospital where geckos ran across the walls and monkeys played outside the windows. The hospital was in a country called Malaysia. My parents lived in Malaysia for three years because my dad was in the Australian Army and the army sent him there.

I came to live in Australia when I was two, and my parents and brother and I lived with my grandparents and aunty in a big double-storey house near the sea. Like Daisy, we had lots of pets. A few years later my little sister was born, and I took care of her the way Daisy takes care of Flora. Even though Daisy's life was very different to mine, and very different to yours today, the one thing that never changes for Australian girls is the importance of family.

HOW I BECAME AN AUSTRALIAN GIRL

by Lucia Masciullo

I was born and grew up in Italy, a beautiful country to visit, but also a difficult country to live in for new generations.

In 2006, I packed up my suitcase and I left Italy with the man I love. We bet on Australia. I didn't know much about Australia before coming – I was just looking for new opportunities, I guess.

And I liked it right from the beginning! Australian people are resourceful, open-minded and always with a smile on their faces. I think all Australians keep in their blood a bit of the pioneer heritage, regardless of their own birthplace.

Here I began a new life and now I'm doing what I always dreamed of: I illustrate stories. Here is the place where I'd like to live and to grow up my children, in a country that doesn't fear the future.

WHAT LIFE WAS LIKE IN

Daisy's Time

AFTER the end of the first world war in 1918, Australians rejoiced. Finally, the terror was over and people could get on with living their lives in peace instead of fighting far from home. Although many people had died, the lucky ones came back to the people they loved. They built houses, bought cars and enjoyed living well after the hardship of the war.

Unfortunately, these happy times did not last very long. In 1929, on a day known now as Black Tuesday, the American stock market collapsed, marking the start of a time where there was little money for lots of people. It affected the whole world's way of life and people who had been living in comfort were soon struggling to make ends meet. Many lost their businesses and many more lost their jobs and homes. All over the world people sank into lives of poverty. This time became known as 'the Great Depression'.

Australia wasn't spared. By 1932, one out of every three working Australians was unemployed. Lots of men had to leave their families and search for work elsewhere. Often travelling on foot, they would roam around the country, picking up whatever jobs they could so they were able to send money home to their families. Melbourne was suddenly much emptier than normal, as many people left the city in search of farm labour.

It took many years for Australians to recover from these hard times, but by 1939 things were mostly back to normal. Unfortunately, just as life was getting better, the second world war was beginning in Europe. The first half of the twentieth century was a very tumultuous time!

Flinders Street Station

This is what the centre of Melbourne would have looked like when Daisy arrived. Compared to how it is today, it seems very quiet and uncrowded. But the cars, trams and people would have been a real shock to a country girl!

DID YOU KNOW THAT IN 1930 . . .

The planet Pluto was discovered by Clyde
W. Tombaugh, an assistant at the Lowell
Observatory in Flagstaff, Arizona.

On April 18th, BBC Radio famously reported
that, 'There is no news.'

Australian cricketer Donald Bradman
scored a world record 309 runs in one day.

Fiddlesticks, the first movie cartoon to
have sound and colour, was created.

The first telephone connection between
Australia and England went into service.

Birds Eye frozen food went on sale for the
first time.

Turkish women were given the right to
vote.

Neil Armstrong (the first man to walk on
the moon) and Clint Eastwood (the famous
movie star and director) were born.

Want to find out more?

Turn the page for a sneak peek at Book 2

Dudley Flats

Daisy looked up and down the empty laneway, unsure of where to go.

It was almost dark and there were strange noises coming from a clump of bushes nearby. I'll probably get slashed by a razor gang or murdered by a gangster like that Siddy Kelly, she thought. Uncle Bertie had told her about the gangsters who attacked people on the streets at night with cut-throat razors. She shivered with fear.

Should I knock and see if Aunty May has calmed down? she wondered. Or maybe I should stay here and wait for Flora to get back so I can tell her what's happened? She'll wonder where I've gone otherwise.

There was a low cough behind her, and Daisy jumped with fear as a man walked past her.

'Nothing to worry about, Missy,' the man said. 'Just out for me evening stroll.'

'Oh . . . yes . . . all right, thank you,' Daisy stuttered. Too scared to stay in the dark lane alone any longer, she ran to Mabel and Elsie's house and banged on the door.

'Whoever is it at this hour?' she heard their mother call from the kitchen.

'I'll get it, Ma,' a voice answered back.

A second later, Mabel flung open the door. 'Daisy! What a surprise. Do you need to borrow a lump of sugar or a drop of milk?'

'Can I come in, Mabel?' Daisy asked. And then her teeth started to chatter with cold and worry.

Meet all our Australian girls.

GRACE
1808
An inspiring girl

LETTY
1841
A shy girl

Nellie
1849
A courageous girl

Poppy
1864
A brave girl

Rose
1900
A determined girl

Alice
1918
A creative girl

There's one just like you.

Daisy
1930
A hopeful girl

Ruby
1930
A happy-go-lucky girl

Pearlie
1941
A spirited girl

Lina
1956
An imaginative girl

Marly
1983
A daring girl

Follow the story of your favourite
Australian girls and you will see that there
is a special charm on the cover of each book
that tells you something about the story.

Here they all are. You can tick them
off as you read each one.

Meet Grace	A Friend for Grace	Grace and Glory	A Home for Grace
MEET LETTY	LETTY AND THE STRANGER'S LACE	LETTY ON THE LAND	LETTY'S CHRISTMAS
Meet Poppy	Poppy at Summerhill	Poppy and the Thief	Poppy Comes Home
Meet Rose	Rose on Wheels	Rose's Challenge	Rose in Bloom
Meet Nellie	Nellie and the Letter	Nellie's Luck	Nellie's Greatest Wish

Meet Alice

**Alice and the
Apple Blossom Fair**

**Alice at
Peppermint Grove**

**Peacetime
for Alice**

Meet Lina

*Lina's
Many Lives*

*Lina
at the Games*

*A Lesson
for Lina*

Meet Ruby

Ruby and the
Country Cousins

School Days
for Ruby

Ruby
of Kettle Farm

Meet Daisy

Daisy All Alone

**Daisy in the
Mansion**

**Daisy
on the Road**

Meet Pearlie

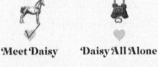

Pearlie's Pet Rescue

Pearlie the Spy

Pearlie's Ghost

Meet Marly

**Marly's
Business**

**Marly
and the Goat**

**Marly Walks
on the Moon**

MEET GRACE
1808

It's 1808 and Grace is living with her uncle in London. They have no money, and Grace is always lonely and often hungry. One afternoon, Grace can't resist taking a shiny red apple from a grocer's cart – and then another . . . Before she knows it, Grace is being chased through the streets! Will she be caught and sent to prison – or worse?

Meet Grace and join her adventure in the first of four exciting stories about a convict girl who is given a second chance.

Sofie Laguna, author of the Grace books, is a highly regarded and award-winning writer of books for children. *Bird and Sugar Boy* was an Honour Book in the 2007 CBCA Book of the Year Awards, Younger Readers, and Sofie's adult book, *One Foot Wrong*, was longlisted for the Miles Franklin Award in 2009.

MEET LETTY
1841

It's 1841 and Letty is on the docks in England, farewelling her bossy older sister who is about to take a long sea voyage to Australia. But then there's a mix-up, and before she knows it Letty finds herself on the ship too, travelling to New South Wales! How will Letty manage when her sister doesn't even want her on the ship? And what will it be like on the other side of the world?

Meet Letty and join her adventure in the first of four exciting stories about a free-settler girl and her new life in a far-off land.

Alison Lloyd, author of the Letty books, is the popular and highly regarded author of several books for children, including *Year of the Tiger* and *Wicked Warriors and Evil Emperors*, a fantastic and fact-filled book about Ancient China.

Meet Nellie
1849

It's 1849 and Nellie O'Neill is arriving in South Australia on a ship bringing orphan girls from Irish workhouses. Nellie and her best friend, Mary, have left the famine in Ireland far behind, and are full of hopes and dreams for the future. Nellie longs to learn to read, to be part of a family once more, and never to be hungry again. But with no job and no one to turn to, how will Nellie's wishes come true?

Meet Nellie and join her adventure in the first of four exciting stories about an Irish girl with a big heart, in search of the freedom to be herself.

Penny Matthews, critically acclaimed author of the Nellie books, has written junior novels, chapter books, and picture books. Her novel, *A Girl Like Me*, was a CBCA Notable Book in 2010 and won the Sisters in Crime's 2011 Davitt Award for Young Adult Fiction.

Meet Poppy
1864

It's 1864 and Poppy lives at Bird Creek Mission near Echuca. Poppy hates the Mission, especially now that her brother, Gus, has run away to pan for gold. What if Poppy escaped, too? Would she survive alone in the bush? And would she ever find Gus, whom she loves more than anything in the world?

Meet Poppy and join her adventure in the first of four stories about a Gold Rush girl who dreams of a better life.

Gabrielle Wang, author of the Poppy books, is a much loved writer for young people. Gabrielle's recent books include her bestselling Young Adult novel *Little Paradise,* and the very popular *Ghost in My Suitcase*, which won the 2009 Aurealis Award for young fiction.

Meet Rose
1900

It's 1900 and Rose lives with her family in a big house in Melbourne. She wants to play cricket, climb trees and be an adventurer! But Rose's mother has other ideas. Then Rose's favourite young aunt comes to town, and everything changes. Will Rose's mother let Aunt Alice stay? And will Rose ever really get to do the things she loves?

Meet Rose and join her adventure in the first of four stories about a Federation girl who's determined to do things her way!

Sherryl Clark, author of the Rose books, is a prolific and popular writer for children. Sherryl's most recent Puffin book is *Motormouth*, a companion volume to *Sixth Grade Style Queen (Not!)*, which was an Honour Book in the 2008 CBCA Book of the Year Awards, Younger Readers.

Meet Alice
1918

It's 1918 and Alice lives with her big family by the Swan River in Perth, while on the other side of the world, the Great War rages. Alice's deepest wish is to become a ballerina, and when she auditions for a famous dance teacher from London, it seems as if her dream might come true. But then there's a terrible accident, and Alice must ask herself whether there are more important things than dancing.

Meet Alice and join her adventure in the first of four exciting stories about a girl with a beautiful gift in a world at war.

Davina Bell, author of the Alice books, is a West Australian writer and editor who works in the world of children's books. Her short stories have been published in various journals and anthologies. The Our Australian Girl books are her first novels.

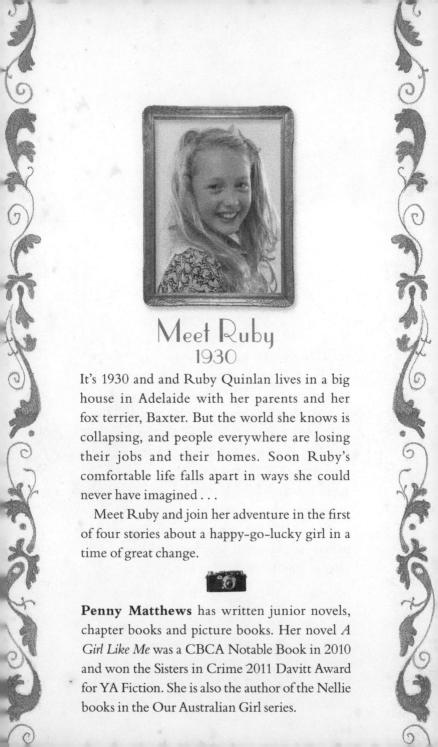

Meet Ruby
1930

It's 1930 and and Ruby Quinlan lives in a big house in Adelaide with her parents and her fox terrier, Baxter. But the world she knows is collapsing, and people everywhere are losing their jobs and their homes. Soon Ruby's comfortable life falls apart in ways she could never have imagined . . .

Meet Ruby and join her adventure in the first of four stories about a happy-go-lucky girl in a time of great change.

Penny Matthews has written junior novels, chapter books and picture books. Her novel *A Girl Like Me* was a CBCA Notable Book in 2010 and won the Sisters in Crime 2011 Davitt Award for YA Fiction. She is also the author of the Nellie books in the Our Australian Girl series.

Meet Pearlie
1941

It's 1941 and the war is changing Pearlie's life every day. Darwin is full of soldiers, there's a spy on the loose, and people are turning against Pearlie's best friend, Naoko, just because she's Japanese. When everything falls apart, will Pearlie be brave enough to stick up for what's right, or will her old fears get the better of her?

Meet Pearlie and join her adventure in the first of four exciting stories about a courageous girl in a world at war.

Gabrielle Wang is the much-loved author of many popular books for young people, including the Pearlie and Poppy books in the Our Australian Girl series. Her most recent novel for middle readers is the lyrical fantasy *The Wish Bird*.

Meet Lina
1956

It's 1956 and Lina dreams of being a writer, but her strict Italian parents have different ideas. Now that she's won a scholarship to a girls school, Lina has other troubles, too. To fit in, she must keep her home life a secret, and even her best friend Mary can't know the truth. But how long can Lina keep her two worlds apart?

Meet Lina and join her adventures in the first of four exciting stories about an Italian girl finding a place to belong.

Sally Rippin is a Melbourne-based writer and illustrator for children of all ages. She has had over fifty books published, including her acclaimed novel *Angel Creek*, and the very popular Billie B Brown and Hey Jack! series.